I0671079

Calling
Dr. Daniels

A "Holy Rock Chronicles" Story

ScanLife

Get more Info About Shelia E. Bell books!

Holy Rock Chronicles
is a series of three short stories featuring members
of the infamous Holy Rock Ministries (*My Son's
Wife* series). *Calling Dr. Daniels* is book one.
These three short stories will be released 60 days
apart. They are meant to give you a behind the
scenes peek at what some of the characters are
doing while I'm busy writing! (smile)
I hope you enjoy this first one. Thanks as always
for choosing to read my work!

Books 1-3
Calling Dr. Daniels
The Woman in Apartment 3D
Ruthless Rianna

Calling
Dr. Daniels

A "Holy Rock Chronicles" Story

Get more Info About Shelia E. Bell books!

NATIONAL BESTSELLING AUTHOR

SHELIA E. BELL

Copyright 2021 © Calling Dr. Daniels, Shelia E. Bell

ISBN: 978-1-7355432-2-2

Library of Congress Control Number: 2021904025

www.sheliawritebooks.com
Aurora, Colorado

Additional titles by Shelia E. Bell
(Some titles may still be found under former name Shelia Lipsey)

Young Adult Titles
House of Cars
The Life of Payne
The Lollipop Girl
The Righteous Brothers

Standalone Novels
Show A Little Love (*out of print*)
Always Now and Forever Love Hurts
Into Each Life
Sinsatiable
What's Blood Got To Do With It?
Only In My Dreams
The House Husband
Cross Road
Forever Ain't Enough

Series Books

Beautiful Ugly
True Beauty

My Son's Wife Series
My Son's Wife: The Beginning (Book 1)
My Son's Ex-Wife: Aftershock (Book 2)
My Son's Next Wife (Book 3)
My Sister My Momma My Wife (Book 4)
My Wife My Baby...And Him (Book 5)
The McCoy's of Holy Rock (Book 6)
Dem McCoy Boys (Book 7)
My Brother, Father...And Me (Book 8)
My Truth, My Time, My Turn (Book 9)
Dem Folk at Holy Rock (Book 10)
Thicker Than Water (Book 11)

Holy Rock Chronicles
Calling Dr. Daniels
The Woman in Apartment 3D

Ruthless Rianna

Adverse City Series
The Real Housewives of Adverse City
The Real Housewives of Adverse City 2
The Real Housewives of Adverse City 3
The Real Housewives of Adverse City 4

Anthologies
Bended Knees
Weary to Will
Learning to Love Me
Show A Little Love (1)

Nonfiction
A Christian's Perspective: Journey Through Grief

Follow me on Amazon bit.ly/sheliabell

Acknowledgements

To all those who have supported my career and continue to support me over the years—thank you. To those who have just taken their first chance on reading my literary work—thank you! I'm fortunate and blessed to do something I absolutely love. When I am weaving and creating stories, I feel like I am living my very own purpose driven life.

Thank you to every book club, every avid reader, every book promoter, and every person who is in the literary arena. An extra special thanks to Rolonda (Frazier) Bridgewater! Rolonda, thank you for your invaluable advice, for being an avid reader of my work, and being one of my top literary supporters.

Extra special thanks and appreciation always to Regina (Robinette) Fleming-Dobbins, Quandra' Swayze, and Carolyn Denise Rooks. Readers and supporters like you make what I do worthwhile and help me to be successful!

Shelia E. Bell

1

"If you want to be successful in this world, you have to follow your passion, not a paycheck." Jen Welter

"Calling Dr. Daniels. Calling Dr. Micah Daniels to the ER. Stat!"

"I gotta go, babe. I'm being paged," Micah said to Fancy.

He and Fancy McCoy initially met at this very same hospital when her youngest son, Xavier McCoy, was badly injured in a car accident. However, it wasn't until months later when they ran into each other again at Holy Rock, of all places, that they hooked up. It was when Stiles Graham was being welcomed as the new assistant pastor and Micah's pastor was invited to render the message. When he attended the installation services and the banquet afterwards, he was pleasantly surprised to see Fancy. Now that he was no longer in a professional setting, he shot his shot and asked her out. Fancy accepted, and since that day a little less than a year ago, the couple had been enjoying each other's company.

Micah ended the call, stretched, and then sat up on the side of the full-size bed inside the hospital's physicians' quarters. He liked his position as a hospitalist but it still called for some long crazy shifts. Choosing to become a hospitalist was his plan to reduce his stress levels, have more normal working hours, and more time to himself. Things had turned out quite the opposite, and he was just as busy as he was in private practice, but he still loved what he did. Usually, he had to round 15 or 16 patients while being hit with a handful of admissions and emergencies. It could be just as stressful as when he was in practice a few years

1

back with two other internists he'd graduated residency with back in the day.

He splashed a handful of cold water against his face, looked at his smart watch—1:30 a.m. He had been on the phone with Fancy for at least an hour before he was paged. He enjoyed talking to her, a lot. He liked her *a lot* too. If she could settle herself down, stop being so consumed with her sons and her ex-husband, then maybe he and Fancy could build something together.

"Dr. Daniels, you're needed in Exam Room Eleven. Some life threatening stab wounds to the abdominal region," the charge nurse told him as soon as he approached the front nurse's station.

"Gotcha."

Entering the room, he was more than shocked to see the familiar face lying on the bed bruised, battered, and bloody. It was not uncommon for Micah to encounter people he knew in the ER from time to time. It was, however, a surprise when he walked into the exam room and saw his ex-wife, Tavia. A staff of interns and residents surrounded her. Gobs of thick, deep purple blood was on the hospital floor. Micah could see extensive wounds from where he stood.

He began barking a round of orders to the resident physicians as they scurried along. The wounds were deep and from what Micah could see upon closer examination, they could have ruptured a main artery and nerves.

"Get her prepped for OR!" Micah barked. "Hurry!"

Micah followed the gurney to OR. The surgery lasted more than four hours. The patient had a fractured jaw, her eye socket was crushed, a stab wound to her pelvic region, and another one was directly to her right breast.

"She should pull through, but it might take some time. She has some pretty extensive injuries," the surgeon explained. "Her right breast is going to be deformed. We thought we were going to have to remove it, but the plastic surgeon was able to save it. For now, that is."

"Thanks for everything, Pete. I'm just glad she's going to pull through," Micah relayed to his surgeon friend.

"She's in an induced coma so she can hopefully heal without experiencing any major complications. We'll keep her in this state for a few days and then reevaluate her."

"'Preciate it," Micah said before the doctors parted ways.

Micah returned to his ex-wife's side as she lay in recovery. He recalled when they met on a popular dating site. Within a few months of meeting, Micah fell in love and proposed. This was one of only three times he'd been in love, but it was the first time he'd proposed.

Tavia accepted his proposal and the downward spiral of his life began.

2

"The worst thing about being lied to is knowing you weren't worth the truth." Unknown

Micah discovered shortly into his marriage that his wife was a compulsive gambler and liar. When they were married, Micah graciously paid off a majority of her debts. One year later, Tavia was in worse financial shape than she had been before she got married, racking up thousands of dollars in debt. Her bank account was in the negative. Her retail clerk paycheck was gobbled up as soon as she got paid because of the direct deposit which went toward her negative bank balance. The only thing different this time about her situation was she took Micah down with her.

She maxed out two of his credit cards, went behind his back and withdrew money out of his bank account, lied about it, and then pawned several items in the house when she ran out of gambling money.

Micah's once organized uneventful life went into a tailspin when he learned Tavia was sitting on a bed of lies that was made for a prime time television show.

During the course of their three year marriage, Micah discovered Tavia, who said she had no kids, did indeed have a grown daughter. That daughter had a kid, making Tavia a grandmother! That wouldn't have been so bad had she informed Micah of her past, but that lie opened the door to her biggest lie. Tavia was not forty-one years old like she told Micah she was when they first met. She was more like fifty-eight! A full-fledged senior citizen.

4

Learning about her lies and gambling addiction, Micah's affection and feelings waned rapidly, but he was determined for his marriage to work because of the covenant he'd made before God.

He also had to admit, girl looked daggone good to be in her fifties! That had been a tough one for him to swallow, seeing Tavia was finer and more beautiful than many women walking around half her age. She kept herself up, always smelled heavenly, and she dressed like a runway model. Her tan skin was smooth and flawless, her breasts upright and perky, and her tummy flat as a pancake.

As a physician, he had banked a substantial sum of money, but by the time Tavia finished with him, he had more debt than the law allowed. Most of it wasted away on gambling, liposuction, and shopping.

He once loved Tavia but all those feelings were lost when he discovered how much of a con artist she really was. He fortunately got out of the marriage, but not without coming out on the losing end. His credit was practically ruined and he had to start rebuilding his life, bank account, and his dignity, but he forgave her. His faith was solid.

Micah believed Tavia would suffer the consequences of the wrong she'd done but not in this way. The last thing he wanted to see was her in the condition she was in.

He dismissed the unpleasant memories and reflected on the positive things about Tavia. Initially, she was the kind of woman who was attentive to his needs both physically and emotionally. She was a good cook; she loved people; and a freak between the sheets.

He set by Tavia's bedside watching her, studying the features of her face. The bruising and swelling from her injuries made her almost unrecognizable. A fresh outpouring of sympathy flooded his heart. Seeing her lying helpless in that bed, he began praying for her healing and recovery.

After sitting with Tavia for as long as he could, he returned to the hospital floor to attend to other patients.

In the hallway leading back to ER, Micah saw the admissions clerk and stopped her. "Hey, Julie, you got a second?"

"Yes, how can I help you, Doctor Daniels?"

"I was wondering if you can tell me if you know how the patient, Tavia Hilliard, the one with the stab wounds, how she sustained those wounds.

"From what I recall James, that's one of the EMTs who brought her in, said her boyfriend attacked her. I believe he's still on the run, but I don't know for sure. What I do know is she's lucky to be alive; he could have killed her."

Micah nodded. "Yeah, you got that right. Thanks, Julie."

"No problem, Doctor Daniels."

Hearing what happened to Tavia was unfortunate but it didn't exactly come as much of a surprise. The woman had conned and robbed one too many people. He was surprised no one had hurt or even killed her before now. Paying for her sins had finally caught up to her.

Micah headed to see the next patients on his rounds. By the time he finished making rounds, the sun was coming up and he was ready to call it a day, night, morning or whatever. He checked in on Tavia again before leaving for the day. She was resting comfortably.

On his way outside to his car, he texted Fancy. "Leaving hospital. Want to get breakfast?"

Ping. "Sure. Where?"

6

"Cracker Barrel good for you?"

"Cool. The usual one?"

"Yea, U want me to scoop you up or u want to meet me. Ur choice," texted Micah.

"Sure, I'll hitch a ride any time. See u when u get here," Fancy replied with a smiley emoji.

Micah grinned while reading the text. "See you in 15 min."

3

"There is only one happiness in life, to love and be loved." George Sand

Micah enjoyed a delightful breakfast with Fancy. She was funny, spontaneous, and an all-around pleasant person to be around. He was especially drawn to her because of their shared faith and religious beliefs. He was into church just as much as Fancy.

When they finished eating breakfast Micah invited Fancy to go back to his house.

Fancy eagerly accepted his invitation. She enjoyed spending time with Micah just as much as he did with her. Whenever she was around him, she was guaranteed to have a good time. Another thing with Micah is Fancy was beginning to feel like she could really trust him. She had been praying that he didn't turn out to be a dog like Winston or a traitor like Hezekiah. Maybe he really was one of the good ones.

Despite the pleasant times she spent with Micah, Fancy was still in an uproar because of the fiasco wedding of her eldest son, the Reverend Khalil McCoy to Eliana Hodges. All of which had been ruined. They still got married, but the whole wedding was sure to go down on Holy Rock's *one for the record* memories. It was nothing compared to the Jubilee Tragedy a few years back, because that was an unspeakable and horrific event. The wedding disaster was more comical than tragic, but don't tell that to Eliana or Khalil—or Fancy by that matter.

Fancy was still receiving texts and prank calls making jokes and saying cruel things about Holy Rock, Khalil, and his wedding day. Though it had been weeks since the wedding, memes were still being shared on social media.

"Come on, Fancy. Settle down. I don't want you to let anything or anyone interfere with our time together. Everything is going to be fine," Micah said as calmly as he possibly could. "You'll see."

"I hear you, but still I just want to say this was all Hezekiah's doing. I know it, Micah. I told you I saw him at church the day of the wedding."

"Babe, are you sure?" Micah was growing tired of hearing about Fancy's ex-husband, her sons, and all their problems. It's all she had been talking about since Khalil's wedding.

"I know what I saw," Fancy told Micah for what seemed like the hundredth time. "He was in the church vestibule talking to Rianna, the choir director. Something isn't right about that chick either. What was she even doing talking to him? She barely knows him."

"I'm sure your son can handle it, Fancy. Let it go. You know that saying."

"What saying?" Fancy looked up at Micah with furrowed brows.

"If you're going to worry don't pray and if you're going to pray don't worry."

Fancy threw up a hand, dismissing Micah's remarks, and went back into her tirade. "What do you mean, let it go? That's it, Micah, I can't let it go. I mean, how could Hezekiah do something like that to his own son?"

"Look, come on," Micah whispered in her ear while leading her over to a one of its kind teal 11-seat sectional that made the massive living space appear smaller than it actually was.

"Wait here," he instructed, after making sure she was comfortably seated. He turned, looked back over his shoulder at Fancy and then disappeared.

Moments later, he returned with a glass of water and sat down next to Fancy whose head was leaned back against the sofa.

"Here." He presented a pill. "It'll help you relax. And before you refuse, it's only a mild sedative. It'll help with anxiety. That's all."

Slowly, Fancy lifted her head, wiped her red eyes, and then studied the small pink pill before looking at Micah as if for final approval.

"It's okay. I told you, it'll help you relax. I'm a doctor, remember?" He half chuckled.

"Yes, I know. I'm not worried about that. I'm just so pissed. I'm over here upset, about to have a darn mental breakdown, and God only knows what Khalil has been going through. I still can't reach him. I know they're back from their honeymoon, but his phone goes to voicemail and he hasn't responded to any of my texts. Sista Mavis said he's been calling in and checking on things at Holy Rock, but she said he and Eliana were still out of the office. While he calls himself avoiding me, my phone is ringing nonstop. Even Xavier isn't answering me. What is going on?"

At that moment, Fancy's phone rang, stopped ringing, only to start ringing again.

"*Spam Likely*, it says. It's spam all right, and I'm tired of it!" She looked at Micah, swallowed the pill, shook her head, and then her text notifier chimed.

"Ignore it, Fancy, and I'm sure Khalil's straight. Xavier too. Stop worrying. They'll eventually call. Khalil's probably putting out a lot of fires after what went down. Not to mention the man is now a newlywed. He's got a whole wife. He won't have a lot of time for mommy anymore," Micah teased.

Fancy gave him an evil eye, letting him know she didn't find the humor in his remark.

"Look, seriously, why don't you put your phone on VIBRATE or turn it off for a while. Lay back on the sofa. Unless you'd rather go get in my bed." He gave her a knowing glance.

Fancy blushed. She wanted nothing more than to get in bed, not alone, but with Dr. Micah Daniels lying next to her. She needed to forget what the previous weeks had presented.

"Umm, sounds tempting," she cooed. "I think I'll take you up on that offer."

4

"The emotion that can break your heart is sometimes the very one that heals it..." Unknown

The next few weeks zipped by. Things had quieted down in Fancy's household, but folks were still sharing clips from the wedding. Several memes had been made that further embarrassed Fancy, but she'd finally heard from Khalil.

"How's Eliana?" Fancy asked, holding the phone against her ear with her shoulder and standing in front of her bathroom mirror trying to open the pill bottle she held in her hand.

"She's good as far as I know. I mean, she's still embarrassed. Think about it. What was supposed to be the happiest day of her life turned out to be one of the worst. She had people from out of town, her family, friends, and not to mention all the virtual guests. She's still devastated and hurt."

Fancy got the bottle opened, poured a pill on the counter, and then replaced the cap.

"I can understand that, but to walk out on her own wedding was a bit much. I wouldn't have let those heffas ruin my day Anyway, thank God y'all still got married."

"Well, I can't say I blamed her then for walking out. I mean, think about how humiliating that was. Not one, but two women, stand up in the church, on her wedding day, with those lies. I still don't know who that one chick was.

"I don't either. I'd never seen her before, but what about Tori? Did you ever get in touch with her? Is that kid my grandbaby, Khalil? Tell me the truth," Fancy insisted.

12

"I told ya, Ma, heck naw, that kid ain't mine. Neither is the kid that other one stood up and claimed was mine. Tori said she had been put up to do what she did."

"Why though? I don't understand. I didn't even know you were still messing with that girl."

"I wasn't, Ma. Don't you hear what I'm sayin'? I *said* she said she was put up to do that stupid stuff. And you already know by who."

"I know it was your father. I told you that. When I saw him out there in the vestibule talking to Rianna, I knew then he was up to no good. But he really did stoop to an all-time low with this one."

"It's all good. I got something for him. I know God says vengeance is his, but this time, I got to help him out."

"You stay out of trouble, Khalil. You have a reputation to uphold. And you have a wife now too so you need to keep your nose clean. You hear me? Don't go doing nothing stupid. Your daddy is going to get what he deserves. You wait and see."

"I hear ya, Ma. Look, I gotta go. I'm heading to Holy Rock. Got a staff meeting."

"At the church or on zoom?"

"Like I said, I'm heading to the church now, but the meeting is going to be a zoom call. I don't see opening Holy Rock again for at least two or three more weeks. I want to make sure this virus scare is passed. The only person in the front office is Sista Mavis, and she's only coming in part time."

"Right," Fancy said, sighing.

"Oh, before I hang up. Have you heard from Miss Victoria or is she still on the outs with you?"

"We haven't talked on the phone, but I texted her the other day and surprisingly she responded. I asked her how she was doing and she said she was good. That was about it."

"Cool. She has a lot going on too, you know. I know it wasn't right the way she sort of took things out on you but you know how things can go."

"I do," Fancy said. "And I'm not mad at her. Just hurt, but I can't imagine what she's had to go through and what she's still going through with Pepper. And your brother, well, I worry about him and those babies. I just knew him and Pepper were going to make it. I have to keep telling myself God is in control of that situation too."

"That's cause he is, Ma. You have to let all this stuff go. Live *your* life. What's up with you and that doctor guy?"

"You mean, Micah? I'm still seeing him."

"Well, keep seeing him. Especially, if he's a good guy."

"I think he is. I haven't noticed any red flags so far."

"Good for you. Well, I gotta go, Ma. Love you."

"Love you too, Khalil. Oh, and tell Eliana hello."

14

5

"The meaning of life is to find your gift. The purpose of life is to give it away." Pablo Picasso

Micah made his usual rounds. When he arrived at Tavia's room, he lingered longer. She was making remarkable improvement physically. Her mental state, not as good.

"Thank you for coming to see me," she whispered. Her voice remained weak and almost inaudible. She still did not look like the Tavia Micah remembered, but her wounds were healing and some of her bruises were fading.

"I'm just doing what doctors do." He laid a hand on top of hers.

"Whatever the reason, I'm grateful."

"I've got good news."

"What?" she asked. "The bastard who did this to me is dead? That's the only good news you can tell me." Her eyes glistened and her voice became somewhat elevated.

"No, nothing like that. And furthermore, you don't need to think like that. Let the cops and the justice system handle him."

"You and I both know how that goes," she said, turning from Micah.

Micah tapped her hand. "Well, the good news is in a few days you're going to be transferred to the hospital's rehab facility across the street."

"Why do I have to go there? I want to get out of here. I don't want to go to rehab."

"Tavia, you need extensive therapy. You need to learn how to ambulate, get your strength built back up, among other things if you plan on making a full recovery. You do want to get back to living your life, right?"

Exhaling, Tavia looked at him, rolled her eyes, and sighed again heavily. "I guess it won't be so bad. At least, that way I won't have to deal with the mess I've made of my life right now. I won't have to be out in the big bad world."

"It's going to be okay. And if it'll make you feel any better, you have me." Micah squeezed her hand gently. "I mean, as your doctor and friend, of course."

Tavia faintly smiled. "Of course."

Tavia texted Micah for at least the twentieth time.
"Micah, I need you."
"This food is horrible."
"I'm in pain."
"You said you would be here for me."
"Micah? WRU?"
"They're not treating me right in here."
Text after text.

He stopped checking them after the last ping and then he set his phone to SILENT.

"Who is that? The hospital or what? I've never heard your phone go off like that. It sounds like mine," a slightly aggravated Fancy asked, rolling over and out of Micah's arms.

Normally, she wouldn't question Micah about his phone calls or the times when he was suddenly called to the hospital. It came with his profession, and she understood that. But tonight was different. Whoever it was that kept texting and calling had interrupted their lovemaking. She could tell by the expression on Micah's face that it wasn't the hospital.

16

A disgruntled Micah, with wrinkled brow and upturned mouth, shook his head. He hadn't told Fancy about Tavia. That's because he didn't know his ex-wife was going to turn out to be a fatal attraction.

Tavia was texting and calling his phone all during the day. It had been three weeks since she'd been transferred to rehab. Almost immediately, the complaints started. One thing after another, she called and complained to Micah about. The fact she told him she had nowhere to go whenever she got out of rehab added to Micah's concerns. However, he didn't want to take on the full responsibility for her well-being. Then again, he couldn't leave her all alone either. He had to tell Fancy what was going on. With the way Tavia was blowing him up, he couldn't see any other way.

Micah turned over on his side in the bed, facing Fancy.

"There's something I need to tell you."

"I bet there is from the way that phone is ringing and your text is pinging. What's up? You got yourself a chick on the side?" She joked and broke into light laughter.

The last thing she expected of Micah was for him to be a cheater. He didn't come off like that. Not at all. He was quite the opposite. Tall, dark, handsome, mild mannered, thoughtful, honest, compassionate, and an especially darn good lover. She could go on and on describing Dr. Micah Daniels' awesome qualities. She grinned at the kinky thoughts about the two of them that suddenly saturated her mind.

"Seriously, I should have told you this a while back, but, well, I didn't know things were going to get this serious with us."

"And how serious *are* we?"

They hadn't really sat down and discussed their feelings for each other. Of course, it went without saying that they were into each other. Micah wanted to spend as much time with Fancy as possible and vice versa. Yet, they'd never professed or confessed their feelings.

"Well, for me, things are very serious," Micah answered, sitting up in the bed but still looking at Fancy. "Serious to the point where I want you to know I have deep feelings for you."

"And what do you mean by *deep* feelings?" Fancy asked, her heart suddenly picking up its pace. Why was she all of a sudden feeling nervous?

"Deep feelings," Micah repeated, this time gesturing with outstretched hands. "You know what I'm saying."

"Actually, I don't," Fancy said. She wanted to hear the words. She wanted him to tell her just what his so called deep feelings meant. She was too old to be playing kid games. She wanted a man to say what was on his mind. Heck, they were two consenting adults knocking on the door of fifty. What was there to hide?

"What I'm saying is I like you a lot. I can see myself falling in love with you. Hell, I think I already am."

"Micah?" The remaining bit of bedcover concealing her nakedness fell away and she was sitting fully in the bed in her birthday attire.

"I think I'm falling in love with you too. I just didn't want to be the first to say it," she said, and the both of them started laughing.

Micah reached over and pulled her into his own nakedness, smothering her with kisses and then pulling her on top of him until she was straddling his lap. His kisses intensified while simultaneously his hands played her like a fine-tuned instrument.

18

Her gasps of pleasure as he entered her caused him to release his own round of pleasurable sounds.

"I love you," he said hungrily as he latched firmly to Fancy's waist, guiding her up and down as she rode him like that pony song by R&B singer, Genuwine.

"You love me?" Fancy leaned back, looking at Micah, and then pulling herself up in the bed.

"Yes, I love you," he repeated, thrusting deeper and harder.

6

*"The meaning of life is to find your gift. The purpose
of life is to give it away." Pablo Picasso*

"We've been seeing each other all this time and
nothing—you haven't said one single solitary thing.
Now, ohhhh, but all of a sudden today, you have
this...this epiphany. Uhhh and this is *after* we
made love, and then you tell me you have a whole
wife! Are you kidding me?" Fancy screamed,
jumping up from off the bed and throwing the bed
pillows at Micah while hurriedly searching for her
clothing.

"She's not my wife, Fancy! Dang, I told you, she's
my ex-wife. And I didn't think it was important to
tell you, until now. I don't go around sharing
everything about my life with every female that—"

"That what? Every female that you happen to
screw!" Fancy scowled and continued looking for
her clothes. She found one of her shoes, put it on,
then her skirt and put it on.

"That's not what I meant and you know it! What
I'm saying is, I haven't been in touch with her since
we divorced five years ago, and then I saw her in
the ER. She'd been stabbed, practically left for
dead. She was transferred to the rehab adjacent to
the hospital. When she's released, she has nowhere
to go."

"Ohhhh, poor thing. I guess you're the only one
she has, huh?" Fancy pouted.

"Right now, I would say, yes, I am."

"And who exactly did she have before you so
graciously volunteered to play Captain Save a ho?"
Fancy was furious. Unpleasant thoughts of how
she'd been duped by Hezekiah and then Winston

20

saturated her thoughts. She was not going to be fooled by another man, not if she could help it. As much as she liked Micah, might actually be in love with him, she was not about to fall victim to his charm. No way. Not this time.

"I don't understand you." Micah was right on her heels. Where's your compassion? Your empathy?"

"Do you honestly think I'm stupid, Micah? I was wondering why you've been so tied up lately, especially these past couple of weeks. I guess you've been playing Sugar Daddy to your helpless ex. Boy, you can miss me with your lies and fake alibies."

Fancy found her last piece of clothing, put it on, and then started searching for her phone and purse.

"Fancy, just hear me out. I'm telling you, there's nothing between me and her."

"At this point, I really don't care, Micah. I don't have time for drama. I'm too old for this crap." Fancy picked up her purse from off the table in Micah's family room and then shoved past him, heading toward the side door.

"Uh, I guess you forgot you didn't drive."

"And?" Fancy wasn't put off by that fact at all. She pressed the Uber app on her phone, booked her ride, and proceeded to walk out the door toward the sidewalk.

Micah trailed her. "You know you're being ridiculous, don't you."

"*I'm* being ridiculous?" Fancy stopped, turned around, and faced him. "No, sweetheart, you *wish* I was being ridiculous. You *wish* I was your little fool, but I'm not, Micah. I'm nobody's fool. Never again. Now if you don't mind, leave me alone. My Uber should be pulling up any minute."

21

"I'm not going anywhere. You need to stop acting childish. You women are all alike. You pretend like you want a man to tell you the truth but soon as he does, you act like...like this." He extended both hands out toward Fancy, shook his head, and turned his lips up in apparent aggravation.

"Oh, I can handle the truth. The thing is you didn't decide to tell me the truth until you were forced to. Had your little ex not been blowing your phone up you wouldn't have told me a darn thing. You know it and so do I. So, to hell with you, Micah Daniels. Go tend to your little charity case! I will not waste any more of my time."

Her Uber pulled up. Like a whirlwind, Fancy opened the door of the compact sized car and hopped inside. Closing the door just as quickly, she looked forward, not bothering to give Micah so much as a nod.

Micah raised a fist, turned around, and stormed back inside his house. Enough was enough. He may have been crazy about Fancy McCoy, but he was not the one to chase a female. He never had to when he was a young buck and he wasn't about to start now as a full grown, mature ass man. Getting and keeping a woman had never been a problem. If anything, he was too nice of a guy. He learned a long time ago that most women don't like good guys. They say they do, but really they don't. It was why he steered away from becoming seriously involved with anyone again. After his divorce from Tavia, he swore off women and relationships, and put everything into his medical career.

Before Tavia came along and broke his heart, Micah lived a fun, carefree, bachelor lifestyle. He didn't mistreat women but he was known to be brutally honest. At times, that might have caused hurt feelings. Micah reasoned better hurt feelings in the beginning than later.

Micah felt awkward seeing Fancy's jealous outburst. He could understand her being a bit pissed about his timing but her being a Christian and all, he thought she would understand how he couldn't just leave Tavia to fend for herself. Especially if he was in a position to help, and he was.

Micah took his religion and faith seriously. He believed in helping others at all costs. Tavia may have hurt him and treated him badly, but that was in the past. He'd since forgiven her and moved on with his life. He learned to stop questioning God. Being a physician, he saw all too often the miraculous power and awesomeness of God.

After Fancy's outburst, and her storming away, he wondered if he had made the best decision when it came to him and Fancy.

His text pinged. He didn't have to look at his phone to know who it was. He was right. It was Tavia.

"Will you order me a pepperoni pizza?"

"With jalapenos?" Micah texted back with a smiley emoji.

"You know it!" smiley face.

Micah searched through his phone, found the nearest pizza place, and made the order to be delivered to the rehab facility's front nurse's station. The pandemic scare was under control but nursing homes and rehabs were taking extra precautions. They only accepted items for patients through the front office personnel who then dispensed the items.

Micah returned to his bedroom and surveyed the mess Fancy had made. Staring at the thrown around items of bedding and clothing, he slowly started cleaning up. Times like this made him remember why he stayed clear of being involved with someone again. Too much unnecessary drama. He'd had enough of it and had seen enough of it. At forty-seven years of age, he was ready for a more peaceful, laid back lifestyle with no drama. He wasn't ready to sacrifice that for anything or anyone...not even for Fancy McCoy.

7

"It hurts because it matters." Unknown

It had been eleven days since Fancy walked out of Micah's house in an uproar. He hadn't heard from her since. He didn't know if she had blocked his number or not. He had texted her and called her on numerous occasions without a response. Most of his calls shot to voicemail as soon as their numbers connected.

If this is the way she wants it, cool with me, and over some crap too, then so be it.

He wasn't going to give Fancy another moment's thought. He didn't have to be shown more than once when it was time for him to make his exit. There were other things on his mind. For one, Tavia was being discharged from rehab later today.

Micah had made arrangements for her to move in with him temporarily until the apartment she'd put in for became available. She was on several waiting lists for apartments but affordable living vacancies were scarce. Plus, Tavia wasn't ready to be on her own, not just yet. She was still using a walker and wheelchair for mobility and would require a caregiver to come in and assist her with daily activities.

Micah set her up in what could be described as a mother-in-law suite. It was on the first floor of his tri-level townhouse. It was equipped with a double vanity bathroom, a sitting area, a kitchenette, and a bedroom large enough for a master bedroom set. A set of French doors led to a lanai on the back of the house.

"Your place is beautiful. Then again, you always had good taste," Tavia weakly complimented as Micah pushed her into the house.

"Thanks. Your room is back here." He steered her wheelchair to the back of the house. Tavia was highly impressed with the arrangements.

He helped her get settled into her room. Later that evening, he brought her a hearty plate of food, chicken, mac 'n cheese, green beans and yams he had ordered and picked up from one of the local restaurants.

"Here you go," he said, sitting the food on the dinner tray next to her bed.

"Thanks, looks delicious," Tavia complimented.

"Don't think you're going to have all your meals back here in the bedroom. You're going to have to get up, force yourself to be more mobile if you want to get back to doing the things you used to do."

"I know, and I will. It's just hard, but I'm going to do it." She looked at Micah with puppy dog eyes.

"Well, enjoy your dinner," he said and turned to leave.

"Micah?"

"Yes," he said, stopping and turning around to look at Tavia.

"Have you eaten yet?"

"No, my food is in the kitchen. I'm about to go eat now. Why? Do you need something else?"

"Yes, I don't want to eat alone. Eat with me."

"I, well, I was about to—"

"Please, Micah. Just eat with me, and when we're done I promise I won't bother you for the remainder of the night,'" she pleaded.

Micah sighed before saying, "Okay. Let me go get my plate. You need anything while I'm in the kitchen?"

"Uh, some hot sauce. That's it."

"Okay, be back in a sec."

Micah returned minutes later with a dinner tray full of food.

Tavia knew Micah to be a good guy. It was one of the things that drew him to her. That and the fact he was quite easy on the eyes with a charming, magnetic voice to go along with his devilish good looks. She went after him like a moth to a flame when they met. Her aggressiveness paid off because she hooked him within months, and the couple were married. If only she had continued to play her hand right, she would have been in a far better situation than she found herself in with her ex. He'd beaten the daylights out of her all because she refused to have a threesome with him and some other girl. But as fate would have it, who did she see in ER that night other than Micah. She'd been back in Memphis for less than a year.

She met her boyfriend, Everett, on a bus ride from Chicago to Memphis. The two of them hit it off and by the time they arrived in Memphis, they were laughing and holding hands like they were long time sweethearts rather than strangers who'd recently met.

Tavia left the bus terminal with Everett, not having any stable place to go at the time other than with her step brother who barely had a roof over his own head. Plus, it was nothing more than a trap house where drugs were sold out of, seeing that her brother was a dealer and petty thief.

The first few weeks, she and Everett were straight. He got her a job as a server at the same fine dining restaurant where he was the night time shift manager. Besides his violent streak, and the fact both of them drank too much, things went okay between them.

The night he almost killed her they had been drinking all day. The night got crazy real fast when one of Everett's ol' flames knocked on his door.

The girl was good and high, that much Tavia could tell. And she acted like she had something harder than alcohol, maybe some hard drugs or pills because the chick was definitely on some wilding out stuff.

Rather than explain to the girl that he had another woman, Everett invited her in to drink and get high with him and Tavia.

Tavia put up a fuss but she quickly quieted down when Everett slapped her and then took her in the back room and gave her a good dose of coke and some type of pill.

When they came out of the back bedroom, the girl and Everett started making out.

"All hell, naw! What you think you doing?" Tavia fumed, jumping up and going over to the chair where the girl had climbed on Everett's lap.

Tavia tugged at the girl's head full of weave, yanking her so hard until she pulled her off of Everett and down to the floor.

"What are you doing?" Everett yelled. "No need for all that. You can get in on this too," he said, and started laughing while reaching down and helping the girl up off the floor.

"You must be out of your mind!" Tavia snapped.

The girl got up, and right away she approached Tavia, trying to pull her close to her.

Tavia pushed back. "You got me messed up!"

"A little threesome won't hurt. Stop being so stuck up," Everett retorted. "You staying up in here, you got to go with the flow."

"I'm not doing anything I don't want to do," Tavia yelled back.

Everett grabbed her and pulled her down to him until she was a hair's breath away from his face. "You'll do what I say when I say it," he barked. He followed up with pushing her away violently and Tavia fell to the floor.

She managed to get up and tried to run off, but the girl grabbed hold of Tavia's ankle, holding her down and keeping her from getting away.

Tavia kicked and screamed. Everett jumped up, ran up to Tavia and struck her across the face with the back of his hand.

Pulling and tugging at her clothing, he and the girl began hitting Tavia and tried to force her to perform sexual acts.

Tavia continued to put up a fight. When she spotted a knife laying on the nearby kitchen counter, she put all her energy toward getting to it.

Everett halted her and pinned her down on the cold concrete tiled floor where he assaulted her with the girl taking part in the ritual.

Tavia took advantage of Everett when he turned his attention momentarily away from Tavia and he and the girl started making out. Tavia took a chance and sprinted toward the knife.

Everett saw her, got up, and went for her. They tussled. Tavia got hold of the knife and sliced him across his arm.

"Ahhhh!" he yelped but not before socking and knocking her down with his fist. He quickly snatched the knife out of her hand and began stabbing her. The girl took off out of the house, leaving Tavia to fend for herself. That was the most Tavia could remember about what had happened.

She woke up in the hospital. She didn't know where she was but when she did regain consciousness she recognized Micah, her ex-husband.

Tavia was well taken care of while living with Micah. She didn't want for anything, and the care she was receiving from the nurses was above excellent. Then again that was the kind of fellow Micah Daniels was.

Tavia was recuperating nicely and was getting up and moving around more than ever. She told herself not to get well too quickly because she didn't want Micah to put her out. She and Micah's paths had crossed for a reason. Now that she had found him again, she planned on staying around.

This time she was going to do everything right. *This* time she was going to play the game right. Who knows what the outcome would be *this* time around. Hopefully, all good.

8

"Hurt me with the truth but never comfort me with a lie." Unknown

Weeks passed and the season was swiftly changing from winter to spring. Micah missed Fancy but he still steered clear of her. He decided it just wouldn't be fair for him to expect Fancy to remain in a relationship with him while he was in the middle of helping Tavia get back on her feet.

As much as Tavia flirted with her ex-husband nothing was going on between them and Micah had no intention of ever trying to rekindle anything they had in the past. He simply wanted to help her while she was down. It was the least any decent human being, any decent Christian would do. That's what his pastor told him when he talked to him about the decision to allow Tavia to temporarily reside in his home.

Turned out, Tavia so far was an ideal houseguest. She still had difficulty maneuvering around the house, but with therapists coming to the home and water therapy weekly at a nearby center, Tavia was making fast improvement.

Micah liked this part of Tavia he was seeing. It was like he was getting to see a whole other side of her. One that was humble, kind, and grateful. He found it easy to help her, but he was still a man, a man who ached for female companionship. He missed Fancy even more. He thought about calling her, but then reminded himself why he had let things lapse between them. Yet, his desire was building up and he wanted to release it with none other than Fancy. No booty call, a for real, straight up, I want to be with you 'cause I miss you call."

31

He didn't say everything he felt, but he did take the plunge and texted her. "Hey HRU?"

He couldn't help himself. It had been weeks since he held her, kissed her, made love to her. He was a man, a man with physical needs. The more he was around Tavia, the more he came to realize how much he missed Fancy in his life.

He waited on a response while he remained in his car before going into the hospital to start his shift. He hoped she would reply before he had to go inside.

Surprisingly, she replied. "good. HRU?"

"I miss u."

"U still have a houseguest?"

"Dang. She would have to ask that," he mumbled. He thought about how he should reply. He wanted to be careful. He didn't want to turn her off. Now that she showed she was willing to talk to him again, he didn't want to mess things up.

"Can I call you later tonight? I need to get into the hospital." He avoided answering her question.

She didn't press the issue. "Ok."

Micah inhaled and then exhaled, relieved she didn't pressure him on it. He then opened his car door. A smile filled his face.

The next few hours went by in a flash. With an increasing number of ER cases and people being admitted, there was rarely a time he could catch a breath.

Finally, the evening slowed to a pace enough where he could sneak off to the cafeteria, grab a sandwich and a cup of strong black coffee, and get

32

off his feet. It was also the perfect time for him to call Fancy.

He dialed her number and patiently waited for her to answer. He was about to end the call when she picked up.

"Hello, Micah. Isn't this a surprise."

"I hope a pleasant one," he said.

"Um, I don't know. Depends."

"I've been thinking about you. I miss you," Micah said, cautiously.

"You *miss* me?" Fancy didn't know how to respond. Was he telling the truth. Did he miss her? Where was his ex?

"Yes, you act like that's hard to believe."

"Actually, it is. I mean, the last time we talked, it wasn't exactly on the best of terms. As I recall you were trying to make me believe some cockamamie story about you having to move your ex-wife in with you because she had nowhere to go and you couldn't bear to see her out on the streets," Fancy spoke sarcastically.

"You've got me there, except it's all true. It's not some made up story. You should know me well enough by now, I would think, to know I'm not the kind of man who steps on other people's feelings. And I definitely wouldn't think of stepping on yours. But is my ex-wife still at my crib? Yes, she is. But believe me when I tell you there's nothing between us. It's platonic. I'm doing what I can to help her. That's it. I'm not attracted to her anymore. That's over and done."

"That doesn't mean she isn't attracted to you anymore. Anyway, let me stop."

Micah smiled over the phone. It made him feel sort of good inside knowing Fancy was jealous.

"I'm glad she's doing better. It was such a terrible thing that happened to her." Fancy wanted Micah to know she empathized with Tavia's situation, but she was also nobody's fool–not anymore.

"She's still on the waiting list for affordable emergency housing, but as soon as the list reopens she should be able to move out on her own. Hopefully, that will be soon. Of course, she'll still need a caregiver to help her for a while," he explained.

Fancy remained quiet, not knowing if she should believe the words Micah was feeding her or not. She had been too vulnerable and naïve way too often in the past. When it came to men, her gullibility was her true weakness. She hated that her heart trusted so easily. That's why she had to be extra sensitive with Micah and her feelings. Here she was again, head over heels for someone who had his own set of baggage, and she wasn't about to help him or anyone else sort out the mess of their life.

She'd done it with Hezekiah and it ended with her spending six years in prison. She'd done it with Winston who turned out to be nothing more than a hustler. She'd repeatedly done it with her sons. She was always worrying and doting over them, trying to help them solve their problems or rescue them from whatever dilemma they'd gotten themselves into at the time. She rarely gave herself enough time and attention.

"You there, Fancy?" Micah asked, interrupting her momentary day dreaming.

"Yes, I'm sorry. My mind drifted for a minute. I'm glad she's getting better."

Fancy still felt some type of way for the way things ended between her and Micah. She could understand his need to want to help others. That's what their faith and religion was all about. Then again, it was another thing to trust a man who had been married to the woman he was helping and that woman had moved back into his home. Therein lied the big issue with Fancy. Trust was a huge factor. After being burned too many times, she could never put her all into what a man said.

"All I want to ask is if you would have dinner with me tomorrow. If not dinner then maybe we can meet for lunch during one of my extended breaks."

Fancy thought about Micah's invitation and laughed aloud.

"What's so funny?"

"Oh, nothing. It just feels good to hear from you." She couldn't help it. Her belly was doing all kinds of flips when she heard Micah's charming voice. She wanted nothing more than to have dinner with him and maybe even a little something special for dessert afterwards!

"I'm glad you answered my text this time," Micah replied. "It's not like I haven't called and texted before now. I thought you had blocked me."

"I thought about it, believe me, but then again, I had a long talk with myself."

"And what exactly did *self* have to say?"

"That I should be more thoughtful and considerate of others. Especially now. So many people are falling on hard times financially and health wise. I'm blessed to have family support and to be in decent health. I shouldn't have caught an attitude because you were lead to help someone, even if that someone happened to be your ex."

"You amaze me. I see why I fell so hard for you."

"Micah Daniels, what on earth are you talking about?" Fancy blushed over the phone line.

"I knew you had it in you. You're a tenderhearted person. Granted, I should have told you about my past up front, but well, I just didn't think anything was going to happen between you and me. But it did and I'm sorry I wasn't more truthful from the jump. Will you forgive me?"

"Yes, I forgive you. I guess I was jealous," she said, timidly.

Micah chuckled. "I'm glad to know you were jealous. So, what do you say? Dinner tomorrow evening? Around six-thirty?"

"Okay, you've twisted my arm. Anyplace in particular?"

"Wherever the lady wants to go," Micah answered.

"What about that restaurant we went to on your co-worker's birthday a while back," she suggested.

"Suits me fine. But are you sure you want to go back there?"

"Yes, that food was good."

"Yeah, it was. Okay, I'll see you tomorrow night then. In the meantime, I'm going to get back to work. I'll give you a call if I catch a break later."

"Okay, gnite, Micah. And Micah?"

"Yeah, Fancy?"

"I'm glad you didn't give up."

"Not half as glad as I am."

9

"Going to church doesn't make you anymore a Christian than going to a garage makes you a car."
Unknown

"I'm glad you came." Micah embraced and kneaded Fancy's left hand in his as they walked up the church aisle and found a seat.

"Well, how could I say no? I mean, you've come with me to Holy Rock more than once. The least I could do was to return the gesture by attending yours. And I told you I haven't heard your pastor render the word since Stiles's ordination service and that's been what?"

"Last year," Micah replied, squeezing Fancy's hand tighter.

After the two hour long church service was over, Micah and Fancy went for brunch at a nearby Mexican restaurant. There, they laughed and talked until things turned to a serious topic—Victoria.

"I've made up my mind. I'm going to call her. Maybe she'll answer and maybe she won't. All I know is I miss my friend," confessed Fancy.

"I'm sure she misses you too. Sometimes people don't know how to fix things, you know."

"Yea and that's why I'm going to reach out to her."

"And what about your son and your grandbabies? How are they?" Micah asked.

"They're good. I plan to stop by there later this evening and see the twins. I still can't stand to be around his partner. Ian just rubs me the wrong way." Fancy bristled.

"I know," Micah said, reaching over and patting Fancy's hand, "but people are entitled to live their

37

own lives, Fancy. That includes your son. I know you don't like him being with another man and raising your grandbabies, but it is what it is. We just have to pray for them. And to think that their mother is mentally incapable of taking care of them is a real bummer too," Micah lamented.

"I mean, it's so sad, Micah. Of course, I pray for my son and those babies every day," Fancy said, shaking her head.

"And Khalil? What's up with his situation?"

"He's good. Just trying to settle into married life. I hope it works out for him."

"You don't sound too hopeful," said Micah.

"I'm not. Not really."

"But why?" Micah asked, curious as to why Fancy would say that.

"They've only been married a few months and he's already complaining about her and saying he thinks he may have made a mistake."

Micah chuckled. "He's still a young man. He'll get used to it. He has a whole lifetime."

Fancy laughed too. "Anyway, enough talk about my sons, what's the news you said you wanted to share with me?"

"Oh, yeah, praise report. My roommate slash ex-wife will be moving out next week. Her housing came through."

"That *is* good news! Good for her. Nothing like having your own. That's what my grandma used to say," Fancy remarked.

"Excuse me," an average height, pencil thin, fair complexion white guy with a scraggly black beard said, approaching Micah and Fancy's table. "Uh, I don't mean to bother you, but ma'am, you remind me of someone that was very close to me. Is your name April? April May?"

Fancy looked at the man. He appeared to be older than Fancy's forty-five years. Maybe by five or ten years. It was hard to determine the age of some folks these days. The very ones Fancy guessed to be in her age bracket could very well be way younger than her. People often told her she looked like she was at least ten years younger than what she actually was.

"Uh, no, you're mistaken," Fancy told the man.

"Okay, I..." He looked over at Micah. "I swear you look just like her."

A hard stare was plastered on Micah's face, peeping out the stranger and trying to tell what was up with dude.

"Anyway, I didn't mean to bother you," the stranger apologized again and darted off just as Micah was about to speak up.

"Guess you have one of those faces, huh?" joked Micah, taking one lingering look at the stranger as he exited the restaurant and positioned himself outside the door.

"I guess I do," answered Fancy, taking a swallow of her tea.

10

"It is not the pain. It's who it came from." Unknown

Micah walked through his house whistling. The night before had been the best one he'd had in a long while. Dinner with Fancy led to dessert at her house. Now it was late afternoon, and he was ready to spend another evening with her. He didn't have to report back to the hospital for 72 hours and he was going to make the best of his time off by spending it with the woman he loved.

"Micah," her voice interrupted his pleasant thoughts.

"Here I come," he answered Tavia. She'd been calling him all morning long, the reason he had to rise early and leave Fancy's home and bed.

Micah entered the guest bedroom. Tavia was struggling to stand next to the side of the bed.

"Hol' up. Here I am." Micah ran to her side and skillfully helped her stand upright.

Still a little wobbly on her feet, Tavia reached to her side for her quad cane. Steadying herself, she took one step forward with Micah by her side.

"Take it slow. You're not in a hurry," he cautioned.

"I know. I..." Tavia took another step.

A few minutes later, Tavia was in the kitchen sitting at the table.

"Good job," Micah told her, placing a plate of bacon, scrambled eggs, avocado toast and coffee in front of her.

"Bless this food I'm about to receive for the nourishment of my body," Tavia mouthed before sticking her fork into the fluffy scrambled eggs and putting a forkful into her mouth.

"Ummm, delicious. Thank you, Micah. You still know how to make some bomb ass scrambled eggs," she said and giggled.

"Thank you, madam," he said, shuffling around the kitchen space and cleaning up behind himself.

"Micah, I know I can be a pain in the rear sometimes," she said, taking a sip of her coffee.

The phone rang. He looked around for it, but he didn't see it.

"There it is," Tavia said, pointing to the counter space next to the refrigerator.

Micah looked in the direction where she pointed, and retrieved the phone.

"Hello, yes, this is he. How may I help you?"

Micah listened to the man on the other end of the phone. He looked up and walked toward Tavia. Pulling out one of the chairs, he sat next to her while he continued listening to the person on the phone.

"That's great," he said. "Yes, she's right here. Would you like to speak to her now?"

Micah looked at Tavia while pressing MUTE on his phone and passing it to her.

"Who is it?" Tavia asked.

"The housing authority. Your housing was approved. Here, they want to talk to you. They have a few more questions and then they'll give you your move in date."

Reluctantly, Tavia took the phone. Moving into her own spot would mean the possibility of winning Micah back into her life would be drastically reduced. He was her bread and butter, the same as he was when they were a married couple.

"What's wrong with you? Aren't you happy?" Micah asked when the call ended.

"Yes, of course I...I am," Tavia pretended.

41

"The place comes furnished but we still need to pick up some things for it, right?"

Tavia smiled. "I guess."

"You guess? Come on, Tavia, talk to me. What's going on in that head of yours?"

"It's just that, well, I'm scared. It's been a minute since I've been on my own, you know. I mean, I've always lived with somebody, like a roommate or boyfriend, husband, somebody. Plus, what if he finds me," she said, hugging herself and shivering.

Micah scooted his chair closer and wrapped an arm around her. "Look, everything is going to be fine. You've been on your own plenty of times. This time is going to be the best. And as far as that ex-boyfriend of yours, I don't think he'll be coming back around. He knows he's a wanted man."

Tavia looked up at Micah, "Thank you, Micah. I really don't know what I would do without your help. After the way things ended between us, I don't know how you would still have anything to do with me."

"The Bible teaches us to forgive, Tavia. What happened between us was unfortunate, but it is what it is. Let the past be the past. Today is all that matters, and right now you are getting a second chance to get your life together. God is good."

Tavia teared up. She struggled to get up from the chair. Micah rushed to her aid.

"See, this is what I mean."

"What are you talking about?"

"How am I going to live on my own when I can barely get up out of a chair without your help?"

As he walked beside her while she stood and carefully exited the kitchen, Micah continued to give her some reassurance.

"You'll still have help, Tavia. And you *can* do this on your own. You have a walker, a wheelchair, and your quad cane. You have any and everything you need to be mobile. What do you do when I'm away at the hospital?"

"I mostly use my walker or my chair."

"And that's what you're going to do when you move. Plus, the caregiver will continue to come for another few weeks to help you adjust to living on your own. You got this, Tavia. I have faith in you."

Micah stopped walking and looked at Tavia with that charming smile of his.

Tavia ambled into the family room while still listening to Micah. Walking over to the sofa, she took a seat near the picture window and peered outside. So far the morning was clear and the sun was shining bright, casting a stream of welcoming light into the cozy space.

Micah took a seat beside her. "God is good."

Tavia said nothing, but continued looking out the bare window. Leaning her head against the comfort of the sofa, she relaxed and contemplated her next move.

Ring.

"Hello," Micah said into his phone. He got up from the sofa and walked slowly away.

He smiled, hearing Fancy's voice.

"Hey there," Fancy said.

"Hey, sexy. What's up?"

Fancy laughed into the phone. "Not much, just giving you a call. I was just leaving Holy Rock. Nothing's going on over there."

"Oh, yea? What you got going on now?"

"Not a whole lot, that's why I was calling, I was wondering if you'd like some company," Fancy flirted. "Not now, later this evening. I've still got some errands to run and some things to do around the house."

43

"You talking about *you* coming over *here*?" Micah questioned.

"Uhh, yea, unless, well I know your ex is there so if it makes you feel uncomfortable with her being there, that's understandable," Fancy threw out there. She really wanted to see where Micah's head was at. Was he really over his ex-wife like he said? And what was his ex-wife like anyway? Fancy was itching to find out.

Micah usually came to her house but tonight, she thought she would invite herself to his house, mostly to see his reaction. Since his ex-wife had been living with him Micah hadn't invited her to come over not one single time.

"No, uh, that's no problem. I'd like the company. Tavia is no problem. I told you that," he reassured her over the phone.

"Okay, in that case, I'll bring dinner. Say something from uh Soul Café?"

Tavia strained to hear what Micah was saying. She already had the feeling it was the Fancy woman on the phone. Tavia had heard him talking to her a few times before, and he also mentioned to Tavia he was seeing someone. She tried to convince Micah that him seeing someone was cool with her. After all, their relationship ended such a long time ago, she told him and all she needed now was a little help until she got on her feet. The truth of the matter was she had hoped, after being connected with Micah again, that this was a sign for her that her life could get back on track if she was with him. It was an added bonus that he invited her to stay with him until she could get her own.

The phone call earlier stating she'd been assigned emergency housing couldn't have come at a worse time. Tavia had hoped and prayed that it would take the housing authority an extended amount of time to find her shelter. Of all times, they had been quick, fast, and thorough. Now in a week she would moving from Micah's and into her own apartment.

"Soul Café? Yeah, that sounds good!"

"Okay, text me what you want. If you want me to bring your houseguest something, text me that too."

"Okay, I'll check with her and I'll see you later."

Immediately, Tavia's jealous bug took a huge bite of her confidence. Why did this woman seem to always call when she and Micah were having a moment? Enough was enough. She needed to see what Fancy was all about, especially since it appeared that Micah really liked her.

Micah entered the family room. "Hey, that was my lady friend on the phone. She's going to come over and bring me dinner from Soul Café tonight. Would you like something?"

"Uh, nah, thanks." She paused. "You know, then again, I think I do want something."

'Okay, what would you like?"

"I want whatever their special is for the day. I've never gone wrong with that."

"Okay, today's special it is. Any kind of dessert?"

"Yeah, peach cobbler."

"Gotcha."

What was she going to do? She had to put a plan of action into place before Fancy arrived.

11

"Anger is our natural defense against pain. So when I say I hate you, it really means "you hurt me."
Unknown

Fancy picked up the food order and headed in Micah's direction. The closer she came to his neighborhood, the more jittery she became. Her throat became parched and she found it difficult to swallow.

Fancy turned into Micah's driveway, turned off the ignition, and remained in the car for several minutes trying to compose herself.

She briefly closed her eyes, and inhaled, gripping the steering wheel. It's not like she hadn't been to his townhome before. That wasn't the cause of her anxiety. What bothered her was the fact she was going to a man's house whose ex-wife lived with him! This would be the first time meeting his ex face to face. What was wrong with her? No matter if the reason was platonic or not, this man had another woman living with him and now here she was going up in the house like they were about to have a ménage à trois.

"Come in." Micah greeted her with a kiss. He removed the packaged food from her arms and she followed him into the kitchen.

"Let me help you get everything together," she offered when he placed the package on the counter.

"Okay, thank you."

Micah retrieved plates and eating utensils while Fancy opened two containers filled with vegetables, another container of fried chicken and meatloaf, and began placing the food on the serving dishes Micah provided.

46

After setting the table, he looked at Fancy and this time, pulled his face to hers and kissed her with all the sexual hunger stored inside himself. The deeply sensuous kiss aroused both of them, forcing guttural groans to emanate from their throats.

Standing out of sight around the corner and leaning against the wall for full support, Tavia scowled as a fresh burst of jealousy consumed her until she felt like she could explode.

Fancy jerked when she heard the astounding noise come from outside the kitchen. Micah pulled back too, and dashed toward the sound.

"Tavia!" Micah ran up to her and got down on his knees to help her. "Are you all right?"

"Yes, I'm good. I just lost my balance, that's all."

Fancy appeared beside Micah.

Tavia concentrated on Fancy. Once back on her feet, and with Micah still holding her around the waist, he walked her into the kitchen.

"Come on, I was just about to come and get you for dinner. You have to take it easy, Tavia."

"I know. I know, but don't make a fuss," she gestured and quickly focused her attention on Fancy. "Hello, I'm Tavia."

"Hello, nice to meet you, Tavia. I'm Fancy." Fancy walked slowly in front of Micah and Tavia, and pulled out a chair for the lady as she approached.

"Thanks," Tavia said and took a seat.

"Oh, no problem. And there's plenty of food. I hope I got everything you asked for," remarked Fancy, heading over to the counter where the food was displayed.

"Would you like me to fix your plate?"

"No, please don't. I'm sure Micah will fix it." She eyed Micah. "Right, Micah?"

"You know I got you."

"Okay, but I don't mind. Really, I don't," insisted Fancy.

"I said I'm good," Tavia snapped.

Right away, Fancy raised hands in defense and took two steps back. "I'm sorry, I didn't mean anything by it."

Tavia rolled her eyes and said nothing.

"Dinnertime, needless to say, was awkward. Micah made as much small talk as possible, but Fancy didn't bounce back after Tavia's biting remark. She opted to remain quiet, finish her dinner, and dismiss Tavia's unpleasant disposition.

The more Fancy sat at the table eating and listening to Micah rambling, the more her spirit began to calm. She reasoned Tavia had a lot on her mind with being assaulted by someone whom she once loved and trusted. It had to be rather hard on the woman, and to add insult to injury, she had to move in with her ex-husband. Fancy felt sorry for her the more she put herself into Tavia's shoes.

A loud knock on the front door startled the three of them. Tavia's head popped up and Fancy's head swiveled toward the sound, while Micah swallowed his food and jumped up from the table.

"Ummm, who could that be?" he said.

He went to the door. When he opened it, he recognized the man as the same man who had approached him and Fancy at the restaurant a few days ago. Who was this guy and what the hell was he doing at Micah's place?

"How can I help you, man?" Micah said, irritation dripping in his voice.

"I'm uh, looking for Tavia. She said this was where she was staying."

"You're the dude I saw the other day at Moreno's."

"Nah, I don't think so. Is she here?"

Fancy looked at Tavia who had turned whiter than a ghost. "What's wrong? Do you know who that is?"

"Yes...it sounds...it sound like..." Tavia whispered, clutching herself and trembling.

"Who? Who is it, Tavia?" insisted Fancy, swiftly standing.

Tavia shivered in her chair, not sure what to say and afraid of what to think. "I...I think...I think it's...it's him."

"Him? Him who?" Fancy screamed at Tavia before she could control her mouth.

"My boyfriend. Everett."

At the door, Micah said, "Look, man, I don't know who told you Tavia was here, but you're out of line, man. If Tavia wants to see you, she'll hit you up. But for now, you've got to bounce."

"She told me she was here. I just need to see her for a minute." The man sounded insistent.

Fancy stood several feet from Micah, in between the kitchen and the hallway leading to the front where Micah was still engaged in conversation.

"I said, no." Micah looked over his shoulder. He couldn't believe Tavia had given this man his address. What in the hell was wrong with her?

"Look, I just need a minute. Anyway, I tol' you she called *me*. Tol' me to come ova here. How else you think I knew where she was?"

Micah's jaw flinched back and forth, his anger mounting. He looked over his shoulder expecting to see Tavia but saw Fancy lurking instead. Straining his neck slightly, he saw beyond Fancy and peeped Tavia who had stood from the table and was standing in place looking like she'd just swallowed a canary.

"You told this dude where I live? What's wrong with you?" Micah seethed.

"Tavia!" Everett yelled, barging in and forcing his way past Micah, pushing him violently against the wall, as he sprinted toward Tavia.

"Get your sh..." he cussed. "We're getting out of here!"

Fancy scurried out of the way, taking off up the hallway.

"No, I'm not going with you, Everett!" Tavia cried. She tried pulling back but she couldn't move that fast.

"Call 9-1-1! Now!" Micah ordered, running toward Everett again.

With two giant leaps, Everett knocked Tavia to the side and turned toward Micah.

"You think you can just take my woman and I would do nothing?" Everett slobbed and ranted. "And you think you were just going to walk out of my life and that would be fine?"

"No, no, I didn't think that, Everett." Tavia was scared for her life. Everett had been violently abusing her almost since they first met. One minute he treated her like a queen and the next he was slamming her head against a wall or worse stabbing her.

Flashing and waving a silver gun at the same time raising it in the air, he pointed the gun at Micah.

"Hol' up, man! What are you doing? It doesn't have to be like this," Micah tried reasoning.

"Everett! What are you doing?" Tavia screamed, and reached out toward him. She managed to grab hold of his leg and pulled on him.

He kicked her off.

"I hate you!" she screamed. "Leave me alone! Just go. Please, just go! Get out of here, Everett!"

Everett turned his head and looked down at Tavia. He kicked her again, spat on her, and that's when Micah pounced at him.

The men started tussling. Micah landed blow after blow but Everett couldn't be stopped. He was like a wild man. He punched and kicked Micah off of him while Tavia sunk her teeth into his calf.

A number of popping sounds were followed by hysterical blood curdling screams and then eerie quietness.

Hiding in the back bedroom closet, Fancy shook and shivered, holding her phone in her hand and whispering to the 9-1-1 operator on the other end.

"For God's sake, please send help right away! I think my boyfriend was just murdered!"

12

"That moment when you can actually feel the pain in your chest from seeing or hearing something that breaks your heart." Unknown

"A triple shooting in a suburb in Collierville, Tennessee has left two people dead and another in critical condition. A fourth person who was able to hide from the perpetrator was found shaken but otherwise unharmed. This appears to have been an attempted murder-suicide. More information is forthcoming as this case develops. This is News Channel 17, Jay Hefner reporting live from Collierville Station."

"Fancy, I saw the news! Oh, my God, I'm so sorry this happened to you," Victoria cried into the phone. "I'm coming over there."

"No, Victoria, you don't have to do that. You stay there and take care of Pepper. I'm fine. I'm just glad you called."

"Look, I know I've been stubborn and foolish. I miss you, my friend. And with what happened, I want to be there for you. So I'm not taking no for an answer. I'll be over there as soon as Pepper's afternoon nurse gets here. She should be here any minute."

Fancy exhaled, pleased Victoria was coming. "Okay, thanks, Victoria."

Fancy and Victoria ended the call.

Fancy laid back on her sofa, her mind replaying the horrific events of last Thursday evening. Tavia and her boyfriend, Everett both died, the result of his jealous anger. Everett shot Micah several times,

52

striking him in his head and torso. He was definitely blessed to have survived. After shooting Micah and Tavia, Everett turned the gun on himself.

When Victoria arrived, the friends talked and sipped on a glass of Zinfandel.

"How is Micah?"

"Still in critical condition."

"Have you seen him?"

"No, I haven't been able to see him. I'm not related to him and with hospital restrictions the way they are, I'm basically on the outside looking in. The only way I've been able to know how he's doing is through his pastor. Thank God he knew me and Micah were friends."

"What about relatives or siblings? Do you know any of them?"

"His parents are deceased and I don't know about his siblings. I wouldn't know how to contact them anyway."

"That's messed up."

"It's crazy. I mean, I was falling in love with him, Victoria."

"Stop talking like the man is dead. You're *still* in love with him. And God's going to bring him through this. Watch what I tell you."

"I hope so. I mean, that night was horrible, Victoria. I'm so grateful I was able to hide. God knows if Micah hadn't yelled for me to call 9-1-1, I probably would have still been in the room when Tavia's boyfriend lost it." Tears flooded Fancy's eyes at the thought of what had happened.

"Don't talk about it,'" Victoria said, rubbing her friend's shoulder.

"I *need* to talk about it. If I don't talk about it, I feel like I might explode. I mean I heard the gunshots, ran and hid in the back bedroom closet, and called 9-1-1. I was praying to God the whole time. When I heard those shots, I almost screamed out myself, but I knew I had to remain quiet or else he could find me and kill me. I heard Tavia screaming and Micah yelling and screaming too. The gunshots, oh my God, Victoria, it was horrible!" Fancy cried.

"Shhh, it's okay. It's okay." Victoria pulled her friend into her bosom, rocking her back and forth in her arms. "Everything is going to be just fine," she continued soothing her friend.

Micah lay in the bed in the hospital's trauma unit. He was pretty messed up. A gunshot wound to the head left massive brain swelling and some bleeding. The wounds to his torso were also of major concern as well.

Eyes only, he looked around the unfamiliar space. *Where am I? What happened to me?*

Micah tried turning his head from side to side. Nothing.

Next, he tried to will his arms and legs to move. Again nothing. Only his eyes scanned the perimeter of the space.

He didn't feel pain, not at all. Quite the opposite, he felt a sense of peace. Tranquility. Calmness.

God has not given me the spirit of fear but of power, love, and a sound mind. Why was that scripture playing through his mind like a broken record? Micah didn't fight against it, he let the scripture play on rewind in his mind.

He was alone but he didn't feel alone. He felt a welcoming presence, like a spiritual connection assuring him *all was well.*

54

Finally, he closed his eyes. Then like a movie screen, like he was floating in mid-air, he opened his eyes and saw his body lying in the hospital bed. His face was grossly swollen, and bandages covered most of the right side of his head. He was almost unrecognizable, but he knew he was seeing himself.

Who would believe this was happening to him? He didn't even know what was going on.

Next, Micah watched as the door to his hospital room flew open. He saw nurses and doctors rush into the room and began zipping around. A machine was buzzing and staff scrambled around his bed. He saw their mouths moving frantically but he was unable to determine what any of them were saying, and strangely he didn't seem to care. No matter what was going on, it didn't matter to Micah. He was experiencing indescribable peace and contentment. He was not fearful or afraid. He was *ready*.

13

"One of the most courageous decisions you'll ever make is to finally let go of what is hurting your heart and soul." Unknown

"Ma, I'm so sorry," said Khalil.

"Me too, Ma," expressed Xavier.

Fancy was numb. The news about Micah's death had taken her totally by surprise. The last she heard, just hours before, from his pastor was Micah was doing better. He was still nonverbal, but he was in and out of consciousness, and the physicians were hopeful that the brain swelling would soon subside.

Later that same afternoon was when Micah's condition went from zero to one hundred. He suffered a massive brain aneurysm which brought on a stroke. He did not survive.

Three lives tragically and senselessly gone, snuffed out, and again Fancy was left feeling numb.

"I want to be alone," she told her sons. "I need time to digest everything what's happened." She cried. "I just can't believe this."

"We don't want to leave you like this," said Xavier, wrapping an arm around his mother's shoulder.

"Xavier's right, Ma. You shouldn't be alone right now. I mean, you just came from the memorial service. That was hard enough. So to leave you by yourself, I don't think is a good idea."

"Look, thank you," she said, looking at Xavier and then at Khalil. "You are such good sons. I love you so much. But right now, I do need some time for myself. These past few days have been torture. I mean complete torture. Sometimes I feel like, well

56

like I don't know what I did to deserve this. I know I've done some bad things, but I prayed and asked God to forgive me," Fancy cried.

Walking away from where she was standing in the kitchen, Fancy walked out of the kitchen and struck out toward the back of the house.

"Okay, Ma, wait. Please," said Khalil. "If you want to be alone, we'll leave you alone. Just call us if you need us. Promise you'll do that."

Fancy stopped, turned and looked at her son. "I promise. Now scoot, you two. Xavier, kiss my grandbabies for me."

The boys left and Fancy made herself a cup of peppermint tea to help her further relax. Sipping on the hot brew, she leaned against the back of her favorite chair and picked up Micah's obituary laying on the table next to her. She learned he had two siblings, both who lived in the Pacific Northwest area. They were at his memorial. Fancy didn't meet them. She was barely noticed among the people in attendance. After all, she and Micah were just beginning to showcase their relationship to Fancy's small circles of friends, and none of his doctor friends knew about her.

Sitting and listening to all the wonderful things said about Micah came as no surprise. It made Fancy feel some type of way though. Why did Micah have to die? Why did it seem like all the good ones got all the bad breaks? She thought she and Micah were going to build something good together, but then his crazy, stupid ex-wife had to come out of nowhere with her crazy, stupid boyfriend and now Micah was dead.

At that moment, Fancy hated everything and everybody. She got up from the sofa, went into her bathroom, and retrieved the prescription bottle. The bottle of pills were first prescribed by Micah when Fancy was stressing out about Khalil and Xavier's drama. She had three refills remaining.

Removing the bottle, she opened it, and took out two instead of one pink pill and popped them into her mouth. Turning on the faucet, she leaned down, cupped some water into her hands, and then put the water into her mouth to wash them down.

The doorbell rang just as she left out of the bathroom.

"Who could this be?" she said aloud. "No one called from the security gate telling me I have a visitor. The boys must have forgot something."

Fancy looked around the family room and kitchen as she passed them on her way to answer the door. She didn't see anything of theirs they could have left behind.

The doorbell rang a second time, making Fancy slightly agitated.

"Hold on, please," she said loudly.

She opened the door. Her hand flew up to and over her mouth when she saw who was standing on the other side.

"What...what are you doing here? How did you get through the security gate?" She suddenly felt flustered. Nervous. Unsure of what was happening.

"Come on, Fancy. You know where there's a will there's a way. All I had to do was follow the car ahead of me when the gate opened."

"That's not as easy it sounds," she said, talking through the glass door separating them. "I haven't seen a car yet that has managed to do that without jamming up the gate or tripping off the gate alarm."

"It can be done. Believe me. But there's another way to gain access," he said.

"And what way is that?" Fancy asked, trying to shield her growing curiosity about why this man was standing at her door unannounced.

"Your sons could have given me the access code."

"They wouldn't do that. You know it and I know it. Next shot."

"Okay, then what if I told you I live in this neighborhood."

Fancy's brows raised. No this man wasn't telling her he lived in in her gated community. That was a lie and she knew it.

"I don't believe that," Fancy retorted, looping her arms.

"Well you should." Hezekiah reached into his pant pocket and pulled out a set of keys, dangling them in front of Fancy.

"I'm two streets over on the back side. On Joy Lane," he said. "Moved in a few days ago unfortunately around the same time I heard about what happened with you. I had to check on you, Fancy." Hezekiah displayed a seriousness on his face and his tone was exact but sympathetic.

Fancy's hand shielded her bosom like she was exposing herself, which she wasn't. Slowly, she unlatched the glass door and opened it, allowing Hezekiah to enter.

"You know I find it strange that you would want to check on me now," Fancy said, turning and walking away from Hezekiah.

"I don't know why you would say that. I've never stopped being concerned about you, Fancy." Hezekiah followed her into the kitchen.

"Yeah, you have a funny way of showing concern for me and for your sons, Hezekiah. I mean, what kind of man who has concern for his family would set out to ruin the most important day of his son's life? Tell me that, Hezekiah!"

"You always were one to jump to conclusions before hearing the whole story. If I did do whatever it is you're accusing me of, you better believe it was only for the good of my son, our son."

Fancy stood at the island, gestured to one of the high back stools for Hezekiah to sit.

He accepted and sat on the stool, resting an elbow on the granite counter top.

"That's bull, Hezekiah! But I'm not going to even go there. Not tonight. I have way too much on my mind already than to deal with you and your mess. Now, tell me the truth. Why are you really here?" Fancy probed.

"I told you. I'm here to check on you. I know you don't believe it, but I still love you, Fancy. That's no bull. And no matter what happened between us in the past, you'll always be my girl. My number one girl." His eyes searched her face, reaching into her thoughts.

"I don't want to hear any more of your lies, Hezekiah. It's not going to work this time." Her eyes were misty and wistful, and there was no denying her attraction. Fancy couldn't break the stare into Hezekiah's hypnotic eyes. Yep, he still had it. Still had that control over her. It was hard, almost impossible for her to describe. All she knew was he had it and she couldn't deny her body betraying her. How could she be having feelings for Hezekiah when she had just hours before been crying over Micah? What in the heck was wrong with her?

The pills began to take effect, making her feel relaxed. She listened to Hezekiah as he went on about how sorry he was for how things went between him and her. She only wished she had been sober and in her right mind to fully grasp what he was saying.

The years since their split had been tumultuous. He had betrayed her on more than one occasion. Why was she even entertaining what this man was saying and why did she even let him into her house? He had hurt her far too deeply, yet if she admitted it, she felt safe and comfortable with him next to her.

"I know saying I'm sorry is never going to cut it. It's never going to make up for how badly I hurt you, but Fancy, that's all I have. I'm not here to try to prove anything to you other than I'm here if you need me, and to let you know I'm right around the corner." At that moment, Hezekiah stood up. "I guess I'll leave and let you get some rest." He moved away from the counter.

Fancy stumbled forward as she took a step. Hezekiah caught her, keeping her from falling. Looking down into her eyes as she looked up into his `, time seemed to stand still.

No longer trying to restrain himself, Hezekiah swooped Fancy into his arms and carried her into the bedroom.

Fancy did not resist. Instead, she snuggled against the warmth of his bareness when they were fully exposed. The hairs on his chest massaged the side of her face. Memories of his excellent lovemaking abilities were resurrected when Hezekiah caressed her face, engulfed her lips with his, and pushed past with his hot blazing tongue.

The fires of expectation quickly grew out of control and passionately she arched her body to meet his. Each thrust was slow, purposeful, and exact.

This was what she'd missed, longed for, ached for. She'd always loved this man. No one would ever know just how much. Memories ruffled through her mind like wind on water. A trembling thrill raced through her. She could never resist him. She couldn't resist him when they first met. She couldn't resist him now.

Clawing her nails deep into his back and drawing blood, Fancy screamed out the name of the man she'd loved since forever. "Hezekiah!"

Epilogue

Rianna paced back and forth across the creaking hardwoods of Apartment 3D. Hezekiah was supposed to have been there hours ago. She'd been calling and texting him and he hadn't responded yet.

Her mind was plotting, thinking about where he was, what he was doing, and who he was doing it with. She sure as hell hoped he wasn't sneaking over to his ex-wife's house. That was the main freaking reason she was against him moving into the same community where Fancy lived.

"I told you it's only until I decide about whether I want to buy another house or not. Plus, I told you, the new ministry is covering the rent and this place is nice."

"Yes, but it's in the same neighborhood as your ex-wife, baby. I don't like that. You know how that makes me feel," Rianna cooed.

"And I told you, you have nothing to be jealous of."

That was a bunch of crock because if that were truly the case, where in the heck was her man?

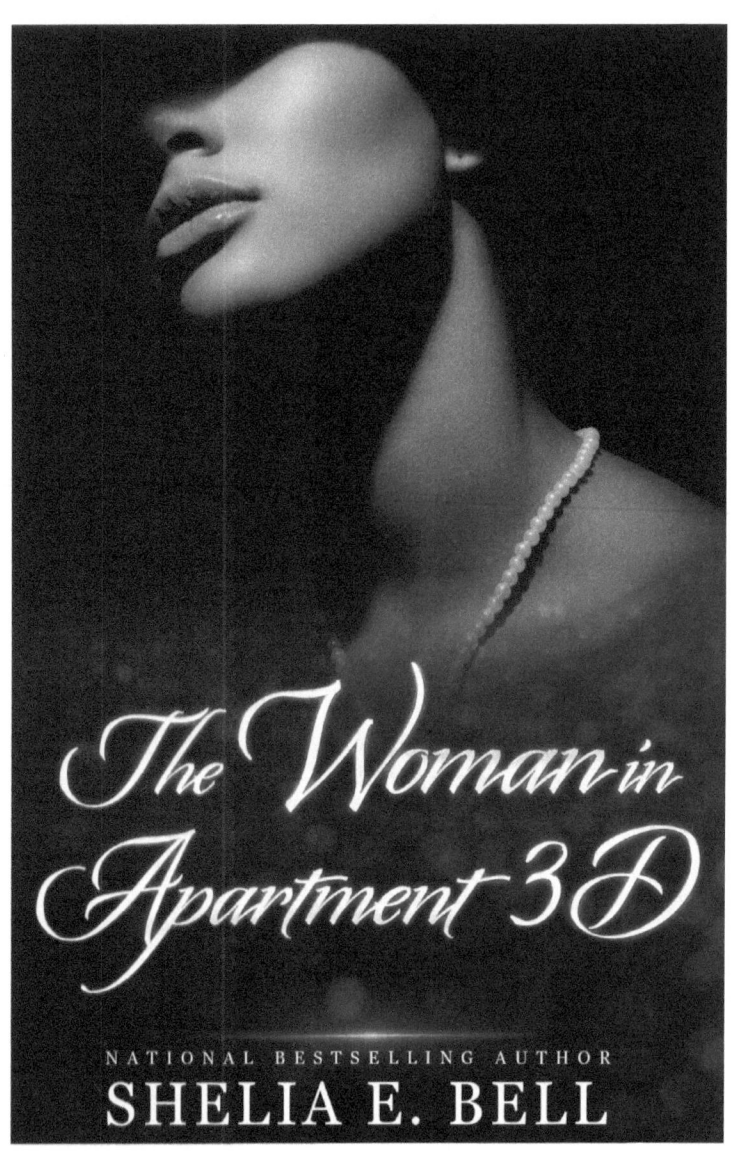

The Woman in Apartment 3D

NATIONAL BESTSELLING AUTHOR
SHELIA E. BELL

Story 2
Holy Rock Chronicles

Words from the Author

Another story down and countless more to go.

In "Calling Dr. Daniels" we see just how twisted and confused a person's mind can be or become. Jealousy, envy, lack, regret and so many other things often play a role in how we behave. It can weigh heavily on our attitudes. *Love makes you do foolish things* is an old saying, but love should never hurt. Love shouldn't make you act foolish.

Even when we encounter hurt, is there ever a time to forgive and forget? For me, this is a tough question to answer, truthfully at least. I can forgive but forgetting is a whole other issue. In "Calling Dr. Daniels," Micah 'forgave and forgot', but what did those actions grant him? Forgiveness can be a slippery slope. Nevertheless, in the Bible, we are commanded to forgive if we want to be forgiven.

I will be keen to hear from you concerning forgiveness after you have finished this short story.

Contact information
www.sheliaebell.net
www.sheliawritesbooks.com
sheliawritesbooks@yahoo.com
www.facebook.com/sheliawritesbooks
@sheliaebell (Twitter & Instagram)
@literacyrocks (Instagram)
@bwabclitfest (twitter)

Please join my mailing list for literary updates and
new book release information
www.sheliawritesbooks.com

If you enjoyed this book or any of my books, please
go to your favorite review site and leave a review!

Follow my Amazon Author Page bit.ly/sheliabell

Other links to my books

bit.ly/sheliaebell
bit.ly/sheliabn

www.ingramcontent.com/pod-product-compliance
Lightning Source LLC
Chambersburg PA
CBHW031900170626

46807CB00004B/1823